The Genie

by M. Hooper

DISCARDED

illustrated by Jessica Fuchs

Librarian Reviewer
Marci Peschke
Librarian, Dallas Independent School District
MA Education Reading Specialist, Stephen F. Austin State University
Learning Resources Endorsement, Texas Women's University

Reading Consultant
Elizabeth Stedem
Educator/Consultant, Colorado Springs, CO
MA in Elementary Education, University of Denver, CO

▼▼ STONE ARCH BOOKS
Minneapolis San Diego

First published in the United States in 2007
by Stone Arch Books,
151 Good Counsel Drive, P.O. Box 669,
Mankato, Minnesota 56002.
www.stonearchbooks.com

Published by arrangement with
Barrington Stoke Ltd, Edinburgh.

Library of Congress Cataloging-in-Publication Data
Hooper, Mary, 1944–
     The Genie / by M. Hooper; illustrated by Jessica Fuchs.
     p. cm. — (Pathway Books)
     Summary: Fudge finds a genie in the box she bought at a yard sale and
plans to use it for a few odd jobs and a birthday present for her father, but her
sister and the genie's misinterpretations make it more difficult than she had
imagined.
     ISBN-13: 978-1-59889-101-0 (hardcover)
     ISBN-10: 1-59889-101-4 (hardcover)
     ISBN-13: 978-1-59889-255-0 (paperback)
     ISBN-10: 1-59889-255-X (paperback)
     [1. Genies—Fiction. 2. Sisters—Fiction. 3. Humorous stories.] I. Fuchs,
Jessica, ill. II. Title. III. Series.
PZ7.H7683Gen 2007
[Fic]—dc22   2006007173

Art Director: Heather Kindseth
Graphic Designer: Kay Fraser

1 2 3 4 5 6 11 10 09 08 07 06

Printed in the United States of America.

Table of Contents

Chapter 1

A Present for Dad?

My sister Sarah and I were at a church yard sale. Our dad's birthday was coming up soon. Sarah and I were both broke, so we went there to find a present for him.

"Hey, Fudge, have you found anything yet?" Sarah asked while we were looking at a table full of junk.

There were chipped mugs, old plastic plates, and rusty tin trays.

"Nothing," I said. "Not a thing."

As Sarah started to explore the next table, I stared at all the junk. Then I saw a small box. It was dark blue, with a silver moon on the top and stars all over. Would Dad like it? I picked it up.

"Do you want that, dear?" said a woman. "It's only a quarter."

"I'll take it!" I quickly replied.

I paid and moved away to look at the box more closely. I lifted the lid. Inside was a scrap of paper with this message:

To call out the spirit of the box, tap G-E-N-I-E in Morse code. To send him back, tap GENIE backward – E-I-N-E-G.

What did that mean?

"What's that ugly thing?" Sarah asked me.

Sarah and I don't get along. She's a year older than I am, and she tries to boss me around.

Sarah smiled. "What do you think I got Dad? The best present! Something fantastic!" She held up a clumsy wire thing. "A book stand for his exercise bike! He's always wanted one."

"Big deal," I said.

"And you got him that old box?" she said. "I bet he won't like that, but he's going to love what I got him."

"Well, hooray for you," I said.

Chapter 2

A Surprise Guest

Two days later, I was sitting at my desk in my bedroom, trying to think about my homework. Over on my bed I had *The Wonderful World of Knowledge* open to the page with the Morse code.

I wasn't planning to do anything about the message on that scrap of paper in the box.

I was doing my homework.

Sarah and I were in the same history class in our school and had the same assignment. We had to write three pages about "Schools in Colonial America." Of course Sarah had already done hers.

I looked at the blue box on my desk and thought, what if there really was a genie? I told myself not to be silly.

Yes, but what if . . .

There was no harm in checking it out.

Before I could stop myself, I picked up the box and went over to *The Wonderful World of Knowledge* to find the letters G-E-N-I and E in Morse code. Then I tapped them on the lid of the box.

I felt silly. I was just about to go back to my homework when there was a sparking noise and a puff of smoke.

There was an odd smell, too, like cheap perfume.

Then a voice said, "Oh, dear me. My mistake. This isn't an ancient Arabian palace."

I jumped. There he was, a fat little man with a bright blue cloak and puffy trousers. He had long pointy shoes with bells on them and lots of gold chains and rings. He looked like a cross between a wizard and a circus clown.

"Who are you?" we both said at once.

He bowed low.

"I am the Genie of the Box."

"Don't be silly," I said. "You can't be!"

"I am," he said. "And you are?"

"Felicia," I told him. "They call me Fudge."

"Princess Felicia?" he asked.

"No. Just Fudge."

He looked puzzled. "I work for princes and princesses most of the time," he said.

He looked around at the mess in my bedroom — the torn wallpaper, the clothes on the floor, and my unmade bed. He seemed even more puzzled.

"I work in grand palaces and lofty castles," he said.

"Sorry," I said. "This time you've got me and 1222 Oak Street. I live here with my sister Sarah and my dad."

"And do you have two hundred servants?" he asked.

I shook my head.

"No room," I said.

This was crazy. It must be some wild, crazy dream.

But at the same time, a part of me was thinking that if he was a genie, wow, how fabulous! A genie could get me things, jewels and gold and a red sports car. Anything! He could take me for a ride on a magic carpet or grant me three wishes.

"Are you a real genie?" I asked.

He bowed deeply. "I am, oh Princess. May your camels never go lame."

Three wishes, I was thinking. A nice present for Dad, some trendy outfits for me, and a mountain bike. That was it!

"Is it true that genies can grant people three wishes?" I asked.

"Of course, oh Princess," said Genie, with another bow.

"Great!" I said. Three wishes! "Can I have them now, please?"

"Just as you desire, oh Princess," Genie answered.

"Thanks a lot," I said. Having a genie around was going to be awesome!

Chapter 3

All the Rage

I was just about to tell him my three wishes when Genie clapped his hands.

There was a big puff of smoke, and just like that, there were three ugly old women in tall black hats in my room.

They had dark cloaks and broomsticks. I almost screamed.

"Here are your three witches, oh Princess!" said Genie.

Each of the three witches gave a horrible laugh.

"By eye of toad and foot of bird . . ." one began.

"Not witches," I cried. "Wishes. I said three wishes!"

"Oh, dear me," said the Genie. "Do you wish to get rid of them?"

"Yes, please!" I replied.

"All three of them?" Genie asked. "You don't want to keep one for spells and magic?"

"No, thank you," I said firmly.

"You'll have used up two of your three wishes, you know," said Genie.

"I don't care," I said, "but please be quick."

One witch was rubbing her hands together. She looked like she wanted to eat me.

Genie looked disappointed, but he clapped his hands. All three of them vanished. There was nothing left but the smell of smoke.

I sat down on my bed, feeling dizzy.

"Do you want your last wish now, oh Princess?" Genie asked.

Just as I was thinking about whether to have a mountain bike or a present for Dad, my door flew open.

There stood Sarah.

She looked at me, looked at him, and yelled, "What's that awful little fat man doing here?"

"He's, um, just a friend!" I told her.

"That's not a friend! That's a genie!" she shouted.

"Can't you do something?!" I said to Genie. "This is my sister, and she's going to make an awful fuss. My dad will find you, and you'll never get back in that box again."

Genie looked at me, and then pointed his little finger at Sarah.

There was a flash and some sparks, and Sarah became silent.

She was still there in the doorway, and her mouth was still open, but not a sound came out.

"What happened?" I asked. "She looks as if she's been frozen or something."

"Almost, oh Princess," said Genie. "I freeze-framed her."

He gave a little bow. "It's the latest thing. Very popular. All the rage with genies right now."

"Interesting," I said.

A Close Shave

I waved my hand in front of Sarah's face. She didn't even blink.

"Do you want her to stay like this?" Genie asked. "It would serve her right for calling me an awful little fat man."

That would be nice, I thought. I wouldn't have her on my back all the time. The teachers at school couldn't say, "It's too bad you're not more like your sister" and stuff like that.

But then it would be hard to explain why I had a sister freeze-framed in the doorway of my bedroom.

"No," I said with a sigh. "You'd better unfreeze her."

"Do you want to go back in time to the moment she opened the door?"

I nodded. "That would be good. Can you do that?"

"We have all the latest tricks," said Genie. "We are most hip."

"But you'll have to go back in the box first, or she'll see you again," I said.

He nodded and gave a bow. "Before I do so," he said, "is there any other job you wish me to do for you?"

"I'm not sure," I said. I didn't want to use up my last wish too fast. "Are jobs the same as wishes?" I asked.

Genie shook his head. "Jobs are just dull jobs," he said. "Like moving palaces over mountains or turning seas into gold. That's what a job is."

"Oh, I see," I said, but in fact I didn't.

Fantastic events might be okay in fairy stories, but they would be hard to hide on 1222 Oak Street.

It was going to be tough to explain where a new mountain bike had come from. And how could I tell Dad that we were going to live in a castle with three hundred rooms?

"Maybe just a small job to start with," I said.

"Could you write me three pages on 'Schools in Colonial America?'" I asked him.

Genie pointed his little finger. There was a tiny flash and a puff of smoke. "Okay. Done!"

"Wow, thanks." I looked over at Sarah, frozen in the doorway. "And now my sister."

Genie pointed. "I'll make that happen in a second, oh Princess," he said. "Right now, just get me back into the box."

I picked up *The Wonderful World of Knowledge*. "Thank you very much. I'll call you up again soon," I said. Just as soon as I've figured out what I want for my last wish, I thought.

I tapped out GENIE backwards on
the lid, E-I-N-E-G, in Morse code. At
once, Genie got smaller and smaller
until he vanished into the box. He left
behind him just a wisp of vapor and
a spark.

A few seconds later, Sarah began
to move.

"What's that?" she said.

"What's what?" I asked innocently.

She looked around, puzzled.

"Um, what's going on? What's that?" Sarah wasn't making sense. "I can't remember what I was going to say."

"It's all that homework you do," I said. "It's bad for your brain."

"Why are you reading *The Wonderful World of Knowledge*? I've never seen you even look at it before," said Sarah.

"There's a lot you don't know about me," I said. "I'm a very private person."

She looked around the room again.

"There's something funny going on in here," she said.

"Maybe you should go lie down," I told her.

"I came in to ask you about Dad's birthday. You're not giving him that old box, are you?"

I looked at the blue box. "No," I said. "I got him something else."

"Well, as an extra present, I thought we could both do some jobs around the house this week," said Sarah.

"Oh, okay," I said. I just wanted her to go. "You make a list."

With Genie around, the jobs would be no problem for me.

Language Trouble

Sarah looked fresh, neat, and tidy as we walked to school. I tugged at my shirt so that it looked baggy. Sarah makes me want to look like a mess.

"Now, here's the list of jobs," she said. "I've circled all the ones I'm going to do."

I looked at her list. She'd chosen all the easiest ones, of course, like collecting the newspapers for recycling.

I had the awful ones like changing the sheets on the beds and dusting the furniture.

I stuffed the list into my school bag.

"Have you done your homework?" Sarah asked.

"Of course I have!" I cried.

"Mine's really good," she said. "I'll get an A+ for it."

"Big deal," I said.

I turned in my homework that morning. Then I forgot all about it until later.

In the afternoon, our history teacher, Mrs. Bloom, was grading our homework, when she yelled my name.

"Felicia!" she shouted. Just like that.

I looked up.

"What's this?" she asked, waving my paper at me.

"Um, three pages on 'Schools in Colonial America,'" I said.

"It could be," said Mrs. Bloom. "But why is it written in another language?"

"Is it?"

"Don't get clever with me, young lady," she said. "You've handed in three pages written in Arabic."

"Oh," I said. I was in a panic. Genie had written my paper, but he'd done it in his own language!

I had a quick idea. "I hurt my hand over the weekend and my cousin wrote it out for me," I lied.

"And your cousin is Arabic?" she asked, crossing her arms.

I nodded. I didn't look at Sarah, but I knew that not even she would rat on me to a teacher.

"And is your cousin two hundred years old?" continued Mrs. Bloom. "This is written in a very old form of Arabic."

"He, uh, my cousin thought you'd like it," I stammered.

"I like homework I can read," she said. "Stay after school every night until you've written your paper in proper English."

* * *

When I got home, I ran upstairs, got Genie out of the box, and told him about the trouble at school.

"I am so very sorry, oh Princess," he said, with a bow. "May all of my camels die!"

"Well, could you just do some little jobs around the house for me tomorrow?" I asked.

"Of course, my Princess!"

"All I want you to do," I said carefully, "is dust the rooms and change the beds. Is that clear?"

"No problem, Princess!"

"Oh, and make Dad a nice birthday cake, too, please."

I tapped him back into the box just in time. Sarah looked in at my door. "Were you talking to someone?"

"No," I said, "I was just saying a poem to myself."

"I heard two voices!" Sarah said with a sniff. "And it smells like smoke."

"I just lit a candle," I said.

"Hmm," she said and sniffed again. "Something very strange is happening around here."

Chapter 6

Jobs Around the House

I was late getting home again the next day because I was still working on my history paper.

Sarah wasn't home. She had gone to a friend's house. That was a really good thing.

I went into the living room, looked around, and gave a yelp. The room had been dusted all right — dusted with gold dust!

It lay thick over everything. The sofa and chairs and even the goldfish bowl glowed with gold!

I ran to my bedroom.

There was a huge new bed with thick wooden posts at each corner and a frilly canopy.

It had an ugly green and gold bedspread covered with jewels.

I rushed to Sarah's room. Her bed was now a big hammock, loaded with fur rugs and stuffed bears at the corners.

Dad's room had a bright blue bed lifted high in the air, on top of four tall marble pillars.

"Change the beds," I had told the Genie. "Dust the rooms."

And that's just what he did.

I ran back to my room and tapped the box.

At once, Genie was there, on my new bed. "Yes, oh Princess!" he said.

"Those jobs around the house!" I said, panting.

"My work is fantastic, is it not, my princess?" he said.

"Oh, it's fantastic all right," I said, "but you've got it all wrong."

I explained to him how you dust a room and change a bed.

"I have to get our old beds back right now," I said.

Genie looked upset. "As you wish, oh Princess," he said with a sniff.

In a moment, I was sitting on my old bed.

"Are all the beds back?" I asked. "And is the gold dust gone?"

He nodded. He was still upset.

I tapped him back into his box. Just then, there was a yell.

"Fudge!" Sarah shouted. "This cake! Where did you get it?"

The cake? I hadn't even looked at it.

"I made it!" I said, rushing down. I went into the kitchen. Shock! Horror!

The cake was almost as big as the kitchen table.

It was the sort of cake you'd make if you had invited three hundred people to a party.

It was covered in blue and green frosting with silver balls and candies on it. On the top, it said, *Birthday Greetings to Father of Fudge, Keeper of the Genie.*

"I don't understand! What's this all about?" asked Sarah.

"Umm," I said, "just wait a second."

I had to run to my room, get Genie out of the box, and get him to freeze Sarah again. Then I had him change the cake into a small one with the writing that made sense, and so on.

Let me tell you, I was worn out.

A Gigantic Problem

"We don't wear outfits for belly dancing to parties here," I told Genie the next day. "It's too weird."

I'd asked Genie to find me an outfit for going out to dinner to celebrate Dad's birthday. The one he chose was made of beads and tassels and not much else.

"But it was a very hip outfit!" Genie told me. "My other princesses like it."

"Well, it isn't right for around here," I interrupted. "And now I have to go and change the goldfish."

Genie's eyes gleamed. "Change it for a shark?"

"Change its water," I said with a sigh. "Goldfish are so boring. I'd rather have a more interesting pet."

Sarah yelled up to tell me that I should hurry down and get on with my chores. So I tapped Genie back into the box and went down.

I was just heading for the goldfish bowl when I heard a noise from up in my room. An odd noise. Like the trumpeting of an elephant.

"What was that?" Sarah asked, looking shocked.

"Was it thunder?" I replied.

"No, it wasn't thunder," she said. "It sounded like an animal."

The trumpeting came again.

"I'll go check!" I said. What had Genie done now? "Maybe my window blinds fell down."

I rushed up to my bedroom, but I couldn't get in. An elephant's bottom was in the way!

"What is it?" Sarah called up to me.

"Oh, uh, our neighbor's cat is in here," I said. "He's been jumping around and, um, making a noise. I'll catch him. Here, kitty, kitty!"

I crawled between the elephant's legs and tapped Genie out of the box.

"What's all this?" I yelled as soon as I saw him. "What is this elephant doing in my room?"

"Not a lot at the moment," Genie said. "It can barely move in here."

"But why is it here?" I yelled. "I never asked for an elephant."

"You wished for a new pet, oh Princess," said Genie. "It was such a large wish that it took a long time to get here."

"But I didn't know I had made another wish!" I said. "And what kind of person has an elephant for a pet?"

"A princess kind of person, of course," Genie said.

"Oh," I said.

The elephant moved its bottom and shoved me across the room.

"Look," I said, "I'm sorry about this, but I'm not a princess kind of person at all. This is not the pet for me."

"Do you wish me to send it back?" Genie asked in an annoyed voice.

"Yes, please," I said, patting the elephant. "It's very nice, of course, but no good in a small bedroom."

"I see," said Genie.

"Fudge!" Sarah's voice came from just outside my door. "Why can't I open the door? What's going on?"

"Nothing! It's okay. I'm just putting the cat out of the window. Here, kitty," I said.

I added softly so that only Genie could hear, "Get rid of that elephant now, please."

Still looking very upset, Genie held up both hands to make the elephant disappear. There was a fizzing sound and a puff of smoke.

I began to tap Genie back into his box. "Sorry," I said to him. "It was a nice thought. But I just don't have room for an elephant."

Genie gave a bow. "Such a large wish," he said. "Anything left of the elephant will go away over the next few hours."

"What do you mean?" I asked.

But he was gone.

"It can't just be the cat!" Sarah said angrily from outside.

And then she fell through the door. She picked herself up, looked around, and screamed.

It was only then that I understood what Genie had said about taking a few hours to go. You see, the elephant's head and trunk weren't gone. They were floating over my desk.

The rest of the elephant wasn't anywhere to be seen.

Chapter 8

Back Again

"It was just a dream," I said to Sarah the next morning.

I laughed. "How could there have been an elephant in my bedroom? Or even a piece of an elephant?"

"It was awful!" Sarah said. "I'm afraid to even go into your room now."

"That's good. Uh, I mean, that's all right," I said.

I sure didn't want her to see what was left of the elephant! Only one ear, a trunk, and half a head were left.

I had an awful time with Sarah the night before.

I had to get Genie to freeze-frame her, put her into her room, and make her sleep. When she woke up, I had to convince her she dreamed it all.

"So many weird things have been going on," Sarah said. "There was that little fat man I saw."

Then all at once she went silent. I was at the sink, and I turned to see why.

My sister was silent because she had vanished!

Just then her friend Ellen knocked on the door to walk to school with us.

I looked everywhere for Sarah, but I knew what must have happened. It didn't take long to figure it out.

I shouted to Ellen that we'd be there in a minute.

Then I ran up to my room (just one elephant ear and one elephant eye were still there) and tapped out Genie.

"Where is she?" I asked. "Where's my sister?"

"She's gone away to think things over," said Genie in a grand voice.

"Gone away? Gone away where?" I demanded.

"She's in the middle of the desert, oh Princess." He bowed.

"It is to punish her for calling Genie an awful little fat man again. She must walk across hot sands for fifty days."

"Then she can come back after that," said Genie.

I shook my head.

"She'll have to come back before that!" I said. "People will find out she's gone. My dad will go crazy!"

"She must be punished, oh Princess," said Genie.

"I'm sure she must," I said. "But my dad will call the police. Besides, Ellen's waiting for us and we have to go to school. Sarah has to come back now!"

I spoke in a bossy princess sort of way. Genie gave a sigh.

He waved his hands a bit.

"Now she is back," he said, pouting.

I said thanks and tapped him into the box.

I went down to the kitchen and let Ellen in.

In the family room, Sarah was watching TV and looking dazed.

"Oh, a show about life in the desert," I said, and switched it off immediately.

"The desert," Sarah said in a stunned voice. "Awful, hot place. You could smell the dry sand."

I felt like dying on the spot.

"What's up with you?" asked Ellen.

"She's just been watching this TV show about the desert," I said.

"Nothing but burning sand," Sarah moaned sadly.

I poked her to get up. "Come on. Time for school!"

Ellen looked closely at Sarah. "Some show," she exclaimed. "You've got sand in your hair!"

I froze, then slapped Ellen on the back. "Very funny!"

"No, really, she does," said Ellen. "There, look!"

I grabbed Sarah's school bag and pushed both of them out of the door.

We had gotten as far as the gate when I made up my mind.

It had been a close call. Too close.

"Just a minute. I forgot something," I said.

I went back into the house and came out with the blue box.

"What do you have that box for?" Ellen asked.

I had decided having a genie was just too much for me to cope with.

"I'm going to drop it off at the church," I told her. "I'm sure they can sell it at their next yard sale."

About the Author

Mary Hooper lives in a little cottage in England. She says her favorite hobby is being nosy, that's what writers call "research." She first started writing short stories after college, and eventually became a professional writer. She has two grown children, Rowan and Gemma, a cat called Maisie, and a green VW Beetle.

About the Illustrator

Jessica Fuchs is a designer, illustrator, and sometimes animator currently living in Burbank, California, where she enjoys tea, fruit trees, and the complete lack of snow.

Glossary

canopy (KAN-uh-pee)—a piece of cloth hung above a bed

cloak (KLOHK)—a cape fastened at the neck

freeze-frame (FREEZ-FRAME)—to make a person stop moving. People often stop a video by using a freeze-frame button.

hammock (HAM-uhk)—a cloth or net hung at both ends as a place to sleep or relax

Morse code (MORSS KODE)—a way of sending a message by spelling words with a pattern of dots and dashes

proper (PROP-ur)—right, correct

tassel (TASS-uhl)—a bunch of threads tied together at one end

trousers (TROU-zurz)—a pair of pants

vapor (VAY-pur)—mist, steam, or smoke that can be seen hanging in the air

wisp (WISP)—a small puff of smoke

Discussion Questions

1. Fudge tries to keep Genie a secret from her dad and sister. Do you think you would tell anyone else about it? If you told someone else, would that make it harder or easier to figure out what to do with Genie?

2. If a genie appeared to you, what would be your first three wishes?

3. Fudge doesn't like it when teachers say she should be more like her sister. Do you have a brother or sister near your age? If so, do teachers and other adults sometimes compare the two of you? How does that make you feel?

✗ <u>Writing Prompts</u> ✗

1. The genie in the story tends to get confused about Fudge's wishes. Write a funny scene where you wish for something but you get something else because the genie misunderstood you.

2. Look up Morse code on a website or in a book. Write a sentence in Morse code using dots and dashes. Give the message to a friend and ask him or her to decode it and write you back.

3. Pretend a genie made you a special birthday cake. Write a paragraph describing the wonderful cake. How does it taste? What are some of the special ingredients? How is it decorated? Will there be leftovers?

✕ Internet Sites ✕

Do you want to know more about subjects related to this book? Or are you interested in learning about other topics? Then check out FactHound, a fun, easy way to find Internet sites.

Our investigative staff has already sniffed out great sites for you!

Here's how to use FactHound:

1. Visit *www.facthound.com*

2. Select your grade level.

3. To learn more about subjects related to this book, type in the book's ISBN number: **1598891014**.

4. Click the **Fetch It** button.

FactHound will fetch the best Internet sites for you!